GROSSET & DUNLAP
An Imprint of Penguin Random House LLC, New York

Adapted by Hannah Sheldon-Dean

Text copyright © 1988, 2019 by The Roald Dahl Story Company Limited.
Illustrations copyright © 2019 by The Roald Dahl Story Company Limited. All rights reserved.
Published in 2019 by Grosset & Dunlap, an imprint of Penguin Random House LLC, New York.
GROSSET & DUNLAP is a trademark of Penguin Random House LLC.
Manufactured in China.

Visit us online at www.penguinrandomhouse.com.

ISBN 9781524793616   10 9 8 7 6 5 4 3 2 1

ROALD DAHL's
Matilda

BE OUTRAGEOUS

BIG IDEAS FROM a SMALL GIRL

ILLUSTRATED BY
STEPH BAXTER

Grosset & Dunlap

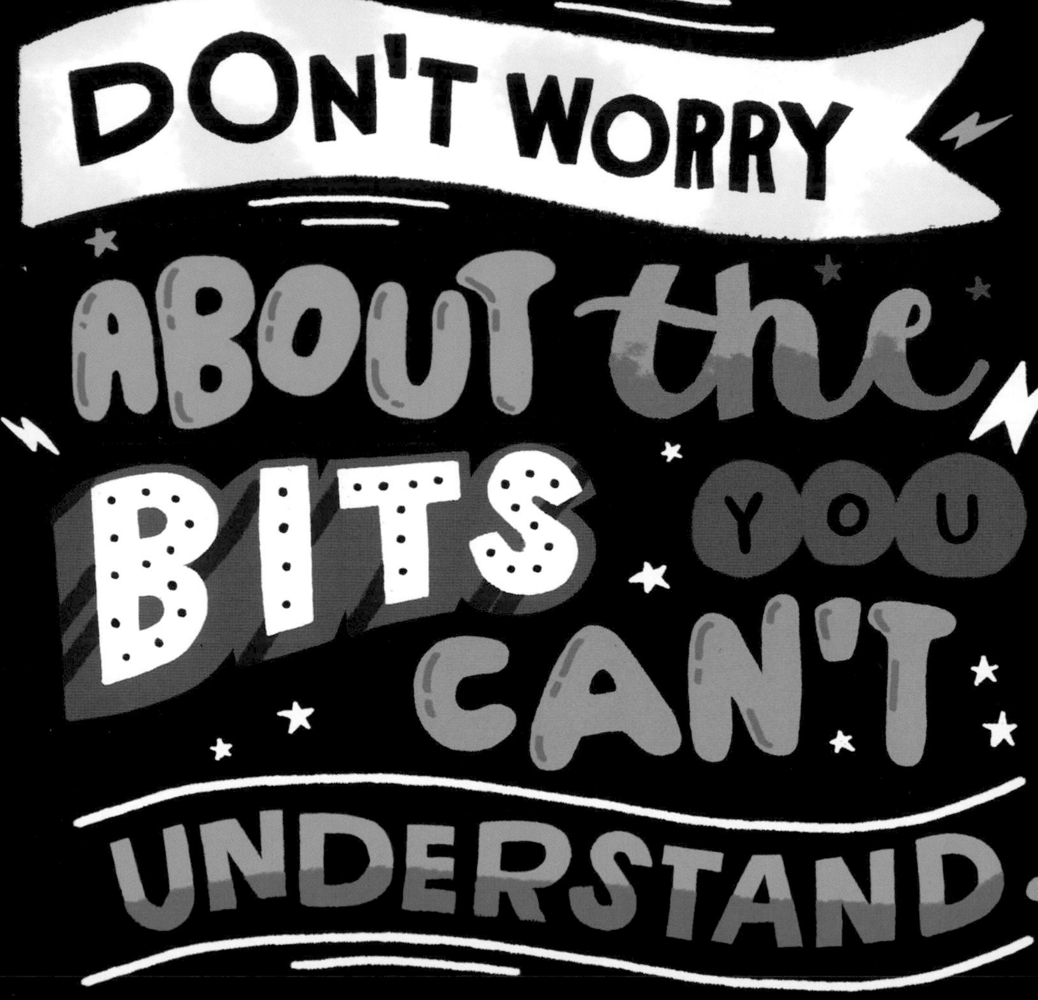
DON'T WORRY
ABOUT the
BITS YOU
CAN'T
UNDERSTAND.

SIT BACK AND ALLOW *the words to* WASH AROUND YOU *Like music.*

WE MAY BE

SMALL

BUT WE'RE

QUITE TOUGH.

THE BOOKS TRANSPORTED HER INTO NEW WORLDS & INTRODUCED HER TO AMAZING PEOPLE WHO LIVED EXCITING LIVES.

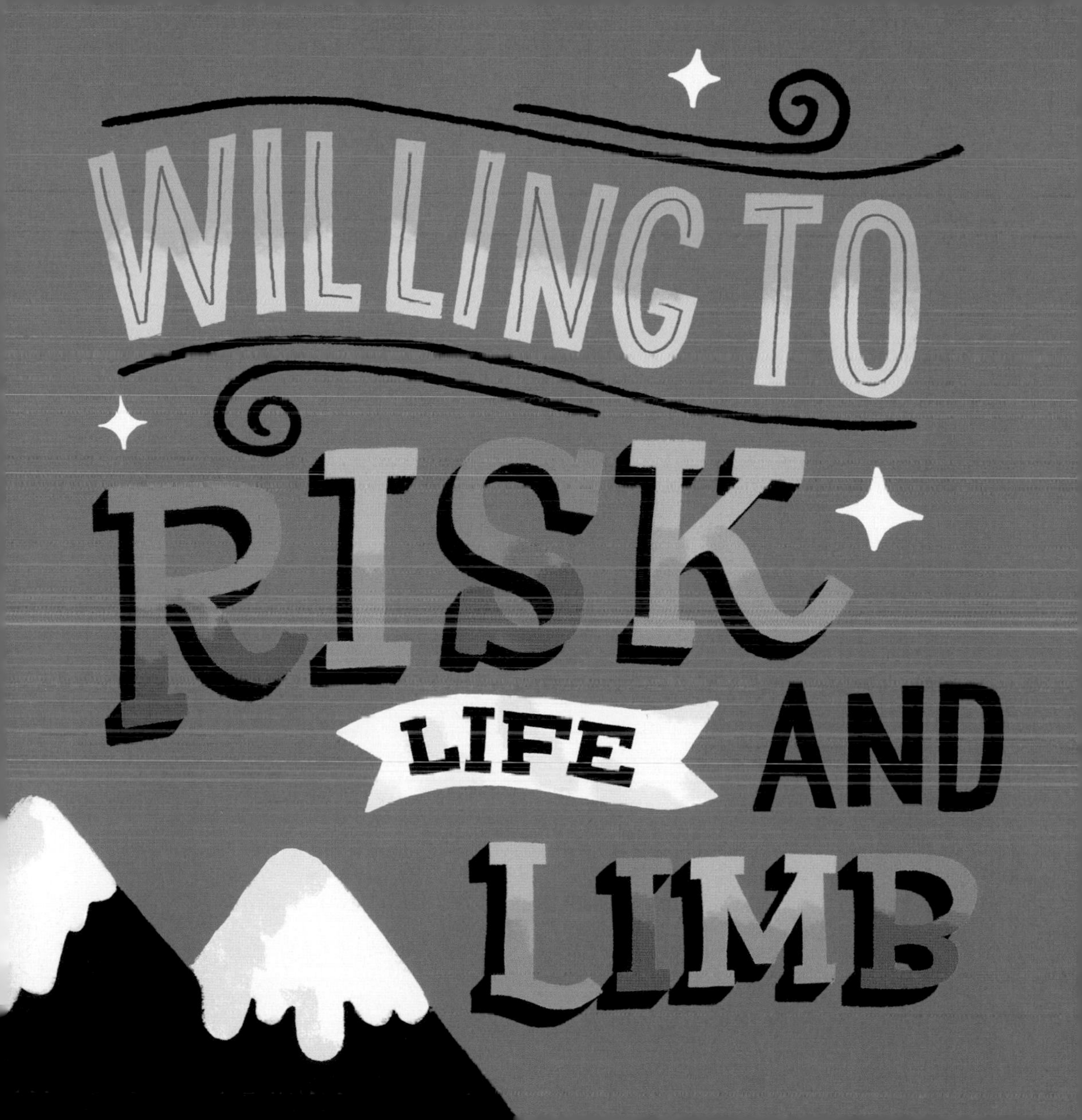
WILLING TO
RISK
LIFE AND
LIMB

A

BADGIRL

IS A FAR MORE DANGEROUS

CREATURE than a

BAD BOY.

WHAT'S MORE,

they're much

HARDER TO

SQUASH.

ALL OF A ★ OF A

SUDDEN

She Found

THAT SHE WAS

FRIGHTENED BY NOBODY IN THE WORLD

NEVER DO anything

BY HALVES IF YOU

WANT TO

GET AWAY WITH IT.

She LONGED TO DO SOMETHING TRULY HEROIC.

ABSOlute amazement

a blaze of silence

AM I A PHENOMENON?

It is quite possible that YOU ARE.